Today Is
The Birthday of the World

Linda Heller
ILLUSTRATED BY **Alison Jay**

This
PJ BOOK
belongs to

_____

_____

Pj Library®

JEWISH BEDTIME STORIES and SONGS

DUTTON CHILDREN'S BOOKS

Today is the birthday of the world.

Today all of God's creatures pass before God, and God asks:

"This year, little giraffe, my dear little giraffe,
Did you eat the highest leaves on the tree,
Happy that I'd chosen you to make a path for the sun?
This year, little giraffe, my dear little giraffe,
Were you the best little giraffe that you could be?"

"This year, little elephant, my dear little elephant,
Did you move the downed tree,
Happy that I'd chosen you to keep the road clear?
This year, little elephant, my dear little elephant,
Were you the best little elephant that you could be?"

"This year, little beaver, my dear little beaver,
Did you build a strong dam,
Happy that I'd chosen you to widen the pond?
This year, little beaver, my dear little beaver,
Were you the best little beaver that you could be?"

"This year, little fish, my dear little fish,
As you swam did you glow,
Happy that I'd chosen you to light the dark ocean?
This year, little fish, my dear little fish,
Were you the best little fish that you could be?"

"This year, little bee, my dear little bee,
Did you fly from flower to flower,
Happy that I'd chosen you to spread their pollen?
This year, little bee, my dear little bee,
Were you the best little bee that you could be?"

"This year, little worm, my dear little worm,
Did you tunnel about,
Happy that I'd chosen you to bring rain underground?
This year, little worm, my dear little worm,
Were you the best little worm that you could be?"

"This year, little cow, my dear little cow,
Did you give your milk each day,
Happy that I'd chosen you to feed so many children?
This year, little cow, my dear little cow,
Were you the best little cow that you could be?"

"This year, little child,
my dear little child,

Did you put seeds in the soil,
Happy that I'd chosen you to plant a garden?"

"Did you paint a big picture and help to hang it,

Happy that I'd chosen you to add beauty to the world?"

"Did you share your toys,
    Happy that I'd chosen you to be kind to others?"

"Did you laugh and have fun,
Happy that I'd chosen you to lift the world's spirit?"

"This year, little child, my dear little child,
Were you the best little child that you could be?"

God waited for their answers.

"Yes," everyone said. They had been the best little giraffe and little elephant and little beaver and little fish and little bee and little worm and little cow and little child that they could be.

"Good," God said, happy that God's creatures had made a path for the sun and moved the tree from the road and widened the pond and lit the dark ocean and spread the pollen and brought rain to the roots and fed so many children and planted a garden and made a beautiful painting and shared the toys and lifted the world's spirit.

"I'm very proud of my dear little helpers.
Because when you are the best that you can be
then the world is the best place that it can be, and
there is no better birthday present."

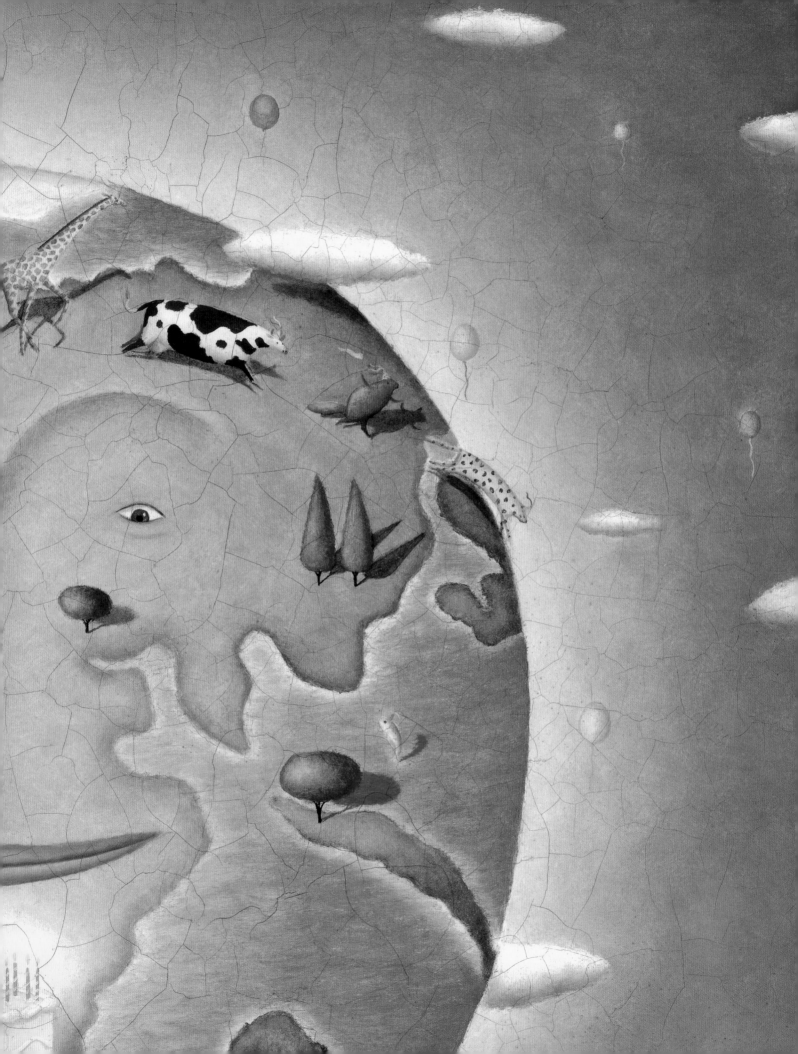

For my teacher George Rohr
and for my friend Donna M. Lippman
—L.H.

For my lovely mum, Maureen. Thank you for being the best.
Love from Alison x

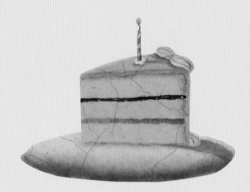

DUTTON CHILDREN'S BOOKS A division of Penguin Young Readers Group

Published by the Penguin Group • Penguin Group (USA) Inc., 375 Hudson Street, New York, New York 10014, U.S.A.
Penguin Group (Canada), 90 Eglinton Avenue East, Suite 700, Toronto, Ontario M4P 2Y3, Canada (a division of Pearson Penguin
Canada Inc.) • Penguin Books Ltd, 80 Strand, London WC2R 0RL, England • Penguin Ireland, 25 St Stephen's Green, Dublin 2, Ireland
(a division of Penguin Books Ltd) • Penguin Group (Australia), 250 Camberwell Road, Camberwell, Victoria 3124, Australia (a division
of Pearson Australia Group Pty Ltd) • Penguin Books India Pvt Ltd, 11 Community Centre, Panchsheel Park, New Delhi - 110 017, India •
Penguin Group (NZ), 67 Apollo Drive, Rosedale, North Shore 0632, New Zealand (a division of Pearson New Zealand Ltd) •
Penguin Books (South Africa) (Pty) Ltd, 24 Sturdee Avenue, Rosebank, Johannesburg 2196, South Africa
Penguin Books Ltd, Registered Offices: 80 Strand, London WC2R 0RL, England

Text copyright © 2009 by Linda Heller
Illustrations copyright © 2009 by Alison Jay

Library of Congress Cataloging-in-Publication Data

Heller, Linda.
Today is the birthday of the world / by Linda Heller ; illustrated by Allison Jay.—1st ed.
p. cm.
Summary: On the birthday of the world, all of God's creatures pass before Him as He asks
whether each has been the best giraffe, or bee, or child they could be,
helping to make the world a better place.

ISBN 978-0-525-47905-5
Special Markets ISBN 978-0-525-42204-4
CIP 081516.6K4/B0722/A2

[1. God—Fiction. 2. Conduct of life—Fiction. 3. Animals—Fiction. 4. Birthdays—Fiction.]
I. Jay, Allison, ill. II. Title.
PZ7.H37424Tod 2009
[E]—dc22   2008034216

Published in the United States by Dutton Children's Books,
a division of Penguin Young Readers Group
345 Hudson Street, New York, New York 10014
www.penguin.com/youngreaders

Designed by Irene Vandervoort   Manufactured in China

5 7 9 10 8 6